The Tiny Baker

written by Hayley Barrett   illustrated by Alison Jay

Barefoot Books
Step inside a story

The tiny baker offers sweets,
A chalkboard list of daily treats:

Puff pastry, custard, caramel
To tempt her tearoom's clientele.

Her customers line up in rows.
Antennae wave well-bred hellos.

They're always elegantly dressed,
Silk gowns or trousers neatly pressed.

They wait to try her lemon tarts,
Her sugar-sprinkled cookie hearts,

To sample her pecan pralines
And nibble lacy florentines.

Before the baker opens up, she straightens out a china cup,

Confirms the pantry is pristine — each surface burnished to a sheen.

Her spotty squad is all-astir. Their whisks are whisking. Mixers whir.

Just as the clock begins to chime,
Her door swings open — right on time.

The baker bows to greet them all,
Then ushers ants, the tall and small,

Straight to her tearoom's pretty chairs.
She mentions her sublime éclairs,

And offers them pink lemonade
Or rose-hip iced tea — freshly made.

But in the kitchen, trouble brews . . .

A fragrant breeze brings flighty news —

The urgent call to swarm away —

Prepare for takeoff! No delay!

The baker, meanwhile, beams with pride,
Congratulates a groom and bride,

Then pats an antling on the head
And goes to check her gingerbread.

She bustles through the kitchen door

To find it in . . . complete uproar!

Disaster struck while she was out. A cataclysmic turnabout —

Her pastry chefs have flown the coop! One red, enormous, dotty troupe.

They ditched their frostings. Dumped their pies.

Forsook their candy butterflies.

The oven's smoking. Kettle glows.
The soufflé batter overflows.

Dark chocolate drips from ceiling fans
And drizzles onto pots and pans.

A sudden noise —

BA-BA-BA-
BOOM!

Reverberates around the room.

The ice cream
maker has exploded.
As some might say . . . it à-la-moded.

A teacup clatters to the floor
As ants rush through the kitchen door

To see her slumped amidst the mess —
Bewildered, flummoxed, in distress,

While sugar drifts like softest snow
Atop her puffy hat below.

Cricket sounds the call to action,

Setting off an ant reaction

To do what ants do very best:

They work together without rest

To clean, to move, to clear, to mend,

To help their tiny baker friend.

They dust her off and stand her up,

Pour her a piping ant-sized cup.

When all is right, they sit back down,
Retrieve their hat or smooth their gown

And sip their sweet rose-hip iced tea
While Cricket chirps his melody.

The tiny baker blinks her eyes.
She shakes her head in stunned surprise.

A half a minute passed, no more.
The kitchen gleams just like before.

No chocolate drips. No sugar snow.
No scorching kettle all-aglow.

No soufflé mess. No à la mode.
No traces of the episode.

"For me?" She dabs a tiny tear.

"For you," they say, "of course, my dear!

"You're our delightful baker chum, and teatime treats aren't why we come.
"Though they're delicious, we agree, it's you we're truly here to see."

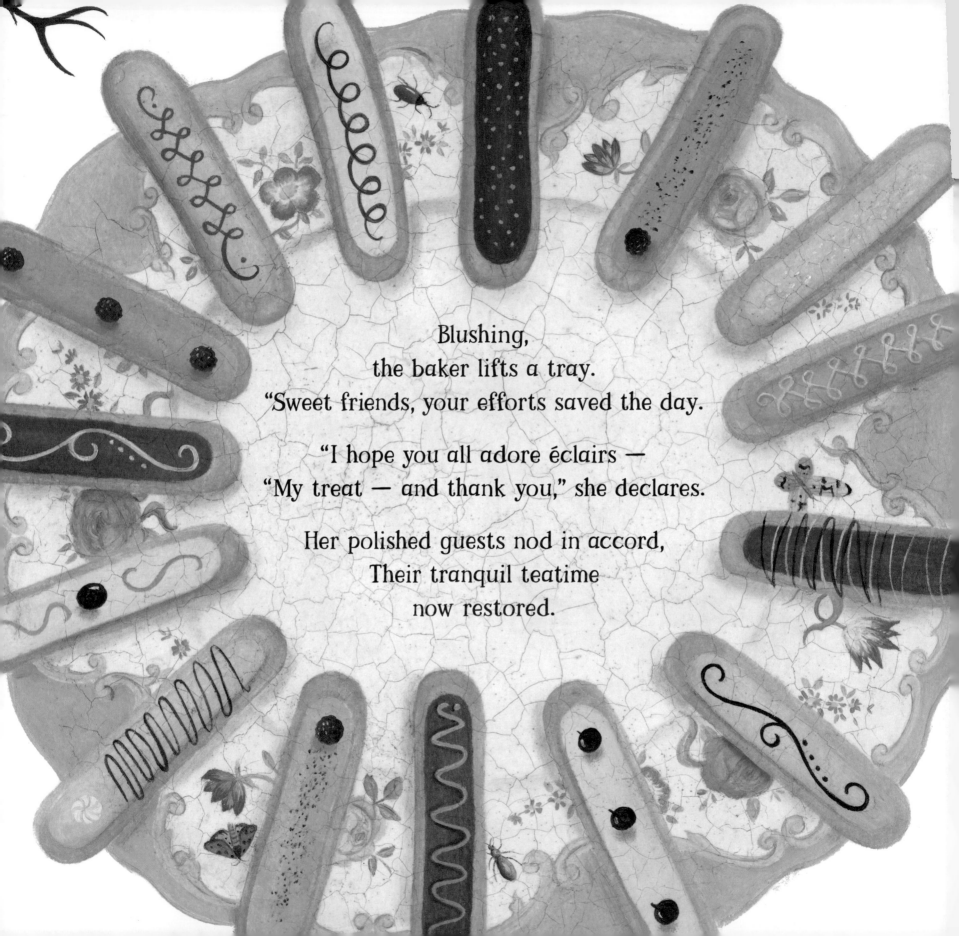

Blushing,
the baker lifts a tray.
"Sweet friends, your efforts saved the day.

"I hope you all adore éclairs —
"My treat — and thank you," she declares.

Her polished guests nod in accord,
Their tranquil teatime
now restored.

Each night, before she goes to sleep,

The baker counts, not woolly sheep,

Hayley Barrett

believes ants are beautiful, admirable creatures and she's just crazy about bees. She often transports roving insects back outside, and she thinks you should, too. Hayley lives outside of Boston, USA, with her husband, John. Their two terrific children have grown and flown, but they come home often for tea and cookies. You can learn more about Hayley and her books, including *Babymoon, What Miss Mitchell Saw* and *Girl Versus Squirrel*, at HayleyBarrett.com.

Alison Jay

has always been fascinated by tiny things, including insects. As a child, she received a microscope and she has never forgotten examining a fly for the first time. Alison is not the best baker, but she does love to make and eat foolproof date-and-walnut flapjacks in her home in London, UK. She has illustrated several projects for Barefoot Books, including the bestsellers *I Took the Moon for a Walk* and *Listen, Listen*.

But friends — true friends — who care enough

To pitch right in when things get tough.